CW00568327

THE LAST DAYS OF
MANDELSTAM

THE FRENCH LIST

THE LAST DAYS OF MANDELSTAM

Vénus Khoury-Ghata

Translated by Teresa Lavender Fagan

LONDON   NEW YORK   CALCUTTA

The author wishes to thank Murielle Szack who provided the
materials necessary for writing this book.

www.bibliofrance.in

This work is published with the support of the
Publication Assistance Programmes of the Institut français

Seagull Books, 2020

Originally published in French as *Les derniers jours de
Mandelstam* by Vénus Khoury-Ghata

© Mercure de France, 2016

First published in English translation by Seagull Books, 2020

English translation © Teresa Lavender Fagan, 2020

ISBN   978 0 8574 2 653 6

British Library Cataloguing-in-Publication Data

A catalogue record for this book is available from
the British Library

Typeset by Seagull Books, Calcutta, India
Ptinted and bound by WordsWorth India, New Delhi, India

CONTENTS

Lying for months—how many?—on a wooden plank, his mattress, Mandelstam wonders if he is dead or still alive.

After the first month, he stopped counting.

Less ill than he, his neighbours might let him know if he is still alive.

But typhus is decimating the camp.

Three out of four deportees are stricken.

A thick stench of sweat, urine, diarrhoea.

Peasant workers or sentenced prisoners, none of the deported know who Mandelstam is. He is the only intellectual in the group.

His neighbour raises Mandelstam's arm when the morning bread is handed out, but keeps Mandelstam's ration for himself.

The poet Osip Mandelstam isn't hungry.

Isn't thirsty.

The poet Mandelstam spends his time listening to the erratic beating of his sick heart.

Forty-seven years old, he looks twice that.

Even dead, his bunkmate would continue to raise his arm to get his bread ration.

Unable to speak, Mandelstam is unable to protest.

His lips quiver, but no sound comes out of his mouth.

He recites the same poem out of fear of dying.

Repeats it even in his sleep and when he manages to dream.

He is in a labyrinth.

He is walking carefully so he won't brush against the walls clammy in the humidity.

A man is following him.

His steps are heavy, deafening.

'You see, I've caught you.'

Mandelstam, turning around, recognizes Stalin by his moustache.

'You will have only my corpse, my poem about you will live on.

'Forbidden from working, from publishing, pursued in city after city, searches, arrests, torture, exile, cold, hunger. You've put me through everything for thirty years, but my poem is stronger than you. Do you want me to recite it for you?'

All we hear is the Kremlin mountaineer
the murderer and peasant-slayer

'Stop. I know the rest.'

Stalin laughs as if it is a good joke.

His laugh shakes the walls, shakes Mandelstam.

'Admit that I frighten you. The proof—you're hiding in a labyrinth.'

'Admit that my poem frightens you, otherwise you wouldn't have hidden me in this labyrinth. But know that I won't retract a single word. Even dead, I will write other poems.'

'—which no one will read. You forget that you are not allowed to publish. No one knows who you are. You have destroyed with your left hand what the right hand has built. All your friends have abandoned you.'

'You harassed them. You imposed your presence at their tables.'

'Slept in their homes though they hadn't invited you, you and your mad wife. Two beggars. Without dignity. You have exhausted your friends. You have worn them out.'

'My true friends are the poor, the starving, who stand in line for a bowl of soup. Those expulsed from their homes, the exiled, the executed. Men, women, children delivered to your manipulating machine.'

Mandelstam shouts out. The shout cracks Stalin's eye. Stalin places his hand on that eye.

The blood spurting from the socket flows to the ground and fills the labyrinth.

Why the labyrinth? he wonders.

Mandelstam knows he is hallucinating.

He tries to latch on to real places and events to erase his nightmare.

So he won't sink.

He has decided to confront death with open eyes.

Going back to the events that led up to his first arrest will help him understand the reasons for his fall.

Having become undesirable overnight, the Mandelstams no longer knew to whom they could turn.

Without work papers, gnawed by hunger, they begged from the few friends they had left.

The alms of a few roubles dispensed by the Writers' Union wasn't enough.

There was no use asking their friend Anna Akhmatova for help, she had also fallen from grace.

Forbidden from publishing, Akhmatova no longer allowed herself even to write, out of fear for the life of her son, imprisoned for attempting to avenge the death of his father, the poet Gumilev, executed without a trial at the age of twenty-seven.

Mandelstam and Akhmatova, the two outlaws.

The only poets who were tolerated were those who bowed down before the regime.

Akhmatova, his childhood friend, his accomplice, named Cassandra in one of his poems, the first to have foreseen the dark years that would unfold over those who dared to say what others were secretly thinking.

Cassandra, sweet-singing Cassandra,
you're moaning, burning—Why
did Alexander's sun hang, a hundred years ago,
shining on everyone?

Exiled in their own country, Mandelstam and Akhmatova refused to leave even when they sensed the danger they were in.

What had I wanted to say? I forgot.
The blind swallow flies back to Pluto's palace
on amputated wings, and plays with transparent souls.
Night songs sing in unconsciousness.

17 April 1934

Arriving from Leningrad, Akhmatova goes to see the Mandelstams on Furmanov Street, in a neighbourhood outside Moscow.

Their room in a communal apartment measures scarcely fifteen square metres.

A mattress, books, two pots, a bucket, mismatched plates and a moth-eaten blanket are all they own.

The room seems less cramped during the day, once the mattress is rolled up in a corner.

Having nothing to eat, Nadezhda goes to a neighbour's and comes back with an egg for their guest.

She is removing the shell when they hear heavy knocking at the door.

A soldier and a man in civilian clothes burst into the room.

They search inside the mattress, pockets, shoes, shake the blanket, scatter papers on the ground, read every line.

They are looking for something specific.

Mandelstam and Nadezhda are petrified.

A friend has denounced them, because only friends know about Mandelstam's poem about Stalin.

All we hear is the Kremlin mountaineer
the murderer and peasant-slayer

Kneeling on the ground, the two men try to decipher everything the Mandelstams have before deciding what to seize.

Letters and manuscripts crammed into a small case, they shove the poet towards the door.

Order his wife not to touch anything they've left. They will be back tomorrow.

Nadezhda has just time enough to give her husband a bag. A change of underwear. He's wearing everything he owns.

Mandelstam has only one pair of trousers, a shirt and a leather coat made from an old suitcase that belonged to Nadezhda's mother.

The couple's two pairs of boots constructed from the same heavy leather give them a stiff, clown-like gait.

Boots indissociable from the three final years of the poet's life.

Imprisoned in Lubyanka, he refuses to take them off, even when he sleeps, wears them during his first exile in Voronezh, then the second in Samatikha.

He also wears them on 27 December at the time of his death in the transit camp en route to Siberia.

Samatikha, then the outskirts of Vladivostok, where night and day trains discharge deportees en route to Siberia. Through a hole in his moth-eaten blanket, the poet who has gone mad from his trials watches those he considers potential poisoners.

He is on the alert. Someone is going to inject him with the rabies virus.

So close to death, the prematurely aged man returns forty years in the past, to his childhood in St Petersburg.

His father, a leather merchant, handling the leather samples in his office looked like he was touching the underside of his skin. His mother's tears were destined for him. His mother cried for him even though at the time he had every reason to succeed. Enrolled in the prestigious Tenischev School in St Petersburg, he came out a revolutionary rather than a budding member of the elite.

Living in Petersburg is like sleeping in a coffin.

—he would later say.

To reminisce facts going back four decades makes a man who is constantly dying, light-headed.

Three weeks without moving, without eating.

A crazy merry-go-round turns in his head.

It would be better not to think of it any more and especially to sleep to calm the increasingly weak beating of his asthenic heart.

Closing his eyes, pressing his eyelids together, doesn't keep away the humiliating scene of his arrest.

Arrested like a criminal by the two men who burst into his room, his eyes are fixated on the egg; he wonders if Akhmatova was able to eat it after he left.

To piece together the scattered remnants of facts going back years, exhausts him.

His feverish mind invents as fatigue overcomes him.

He sees the poet David Brodsky in their room during the arrest even though Brodsky wasn't there.

Brodsky is eyeing the egg meant for Akhmatova; he grabs it, plunges it into salt and eats it while the two men are hustling him out the door.

Dragged by two arms of steel, he still hears his shoes scraping the asphalt on the street.

Where are they taking him, and will they also arrest Nadezhda, who has been sharing his hell for years?

How to explain the sound of bells when bells have disappeared from Soviet Russia, melted down for canons for the years of war. Churches transformed into gathering places, into gyms or hangars in the countryside.

How can he sleep with all those bells ringing in his head?

Because it is sleep, not death; because only sleep can sew back together the destroyed fabric of his rotten heart.

I won't die until my poems are published.

The sad eyes of his bunkmates say the opposite.

Blue lips, skin like parchment, shallow breathing; he is suffocating.

I won't die as long as I can see images.

An apartment emerges from under his eyelids.

A bourgeois apartment in a suburb of St Petersburg.

Parties are held in the large room.

Seated at his desk, the father is examining a leather sample.

The mother is playing the piano. The mother sometimes reads poems to the child.

Heavy features on the man.

Delicate features on the woman.

The man speaks a confused mixture of German and Yiddish.

The woman speaks in a refined language.

The mother speaks several languages.

A toad married to a swan, he would think when he was old enough to judge.

The woman teaches piano. The man is in the leather business. He is a leather merchant.

Tears flow down the face of the woman who is playing the piano although she isn't crying.

There is also the grandmother in her dressing gown with yellow flowers, who knows only one phrase in Russian: 'Have you eaten?'

The Mandelstam family is from Latvia.

The grandfather's bushy eyebrows frighten the child who bursts into tears when he puts him on his lap.

A Jewish family but who don't go to synagogue, don't frequent bourgeois society, nor the aristocracy.

The great-grandfather, a rabbi, translated the Bible into Russian.

The child thinks his father is a writer because of the files piled up on his desk.

He fears his father; he loves his mother.

The child who has a tendency to see darkness everywhere, sees the walls closing in around him as if to crush him. The books on the shelves are only stones fallen from ruins, and the logs that burn in the fireplace a battle between two dragons.

So close to death, he hasn't forgiven the poet Mikoski for calling his mother a stupid Jew.

The Jewish quarter attracted him like a magnet.

The sublime Tchaikovsky symphony sounds throughout the ghetto behind the barbed wire.

Attraction and repulsion. Refusing to be contained in a clan or religion. Enrolled in the Talmud School, the child runs away after the first lesson.

His mother dressed him elegantly, a cloth coat with fur lining—though now he has nothing and it's forty degrees below zero, his coat exchanged for three pounds of sugar that was then stolen from him.

Nadezhda would have given him her fur-lined cloak if the two men who arrested him hadn't promised he would return very soon. 'In just the time it takes to ask him a few questions.'

In his fog, Mandelstam hangs on to meaningless details. He obsesses over his coat exchanged for sugar, the egg eaten by Brodsky when it was meant for his friend Akhmatova.

Mandelstam is going mad wanting to know what has happened to them.

An epidemic of madness afflicted all suspects, all undesirables, all intellectuals.

Mandelstam and Akhmatova when they met whispered like conspirators, whispered their poems. Because only poems that reflected the Party line were allowed.

Writing was considered an act of terrorism, and so the two poets themselves no longer wrote and, above all, didn't keep any writing in their homes.

Scattered among reliable friends, Mandelstam's poems were sheltered from searches.

Incapable of remembering the beginning of a poem, Mandelstam would awaken Nadezhda, who had copied it, in the middle of the night.

Still half-asleep, Nadezhda couldn't remember either.

Going through all the letters of the alphabet was fruitless, so he sent her to friends who kept his poems. Any hour was acceptable for the one who lived only for his poetry.

Deported, tortured, expelled from their lodgings, a great many of the guardians of Mandelstam's poems met a tragic end.

Mandelstam's enemy was the most powerful man in the country.

I've become afraid of living life out—
And pulling back, like a leaf from a tree,
And that I'll love nothing,
And vanish like a nameless stone.

—wrote the one who felt the vise tightening around him, ready to crush him.

Banned from Moscow after his release from prison, the authorities give him twenty-four hours to leave the city. Mandelstam has to choose someplace far from the capital.

He chooses Voronezh because there is an exiled doctor there.

A horse-drawn cart awaits the couple at the train station.

The surroundings are idyllic, but it is infernal in the communal apartment where several families are crammed in together.

The apartment is too noisy. Not a peaceful place where he can be alone and write.

Nowhere to go except the street, while keeping the curfew in mind.

A figure bent over by the wind, Mandelstam walks through the night in the icy streets.

The sound of the poem composed in the dark the same as that of his shoes crunching in the snow. A suctioning sound, the cold and the words are sucking his energy.

He returns exhausted from his wanderings, and joins Nadezhda under their moth-eaten blanket, reciting the poem written in his head. Nadezhda collects the words like breadcrumbs from a feast, transcribes them, waits for daylight to distribute them among the trustworthy.

Under their blanket, Mandelstam and Nadezhda meld into each other to stay warm, to be ONE.

'You will be called Stalinette,' he teased her.

Ten years younger than he, the young woman embraced the demands of the man she had married in Kiev after falling madly in love when they first met.

To eat, to be clothed, to be warm, those were Nadezhda's only concerns. She forgot she was a woman, fixed her hair without looking in a mirror, wore the same dress for years.

Worn out, the dress became a skirt while waiting for a charitable friend to replace it.

Exiled, prohibited from working, Mandelstam couldn't earn a living. Nadezhda earned the two hundred roubles needed to pay the rent on their room by translating bad novels.

'Profession—beggars,' he claimed with bravado despite the shame that devoured him, and he sent his young wife to beg from the few friends who hadn't abandoned them.

Sometimes the couple would argue, but never about money, always for a poem that had gone missing.

Would they have to take the pillow apart to find it?

Should they ask their friends who kept copies?

Two animals in their den. Mandelstam and Nadezhda would eat when they found something to eat while the Pasternaks had real meals, real dishes, rugs, curtains and children, and the Party poets wore three-piece suits, rode in cars with chauffeurs, lived in flats.

Terrible winters in Voronezh. Not enough coal for heat, no money to eat. Eating chickpeas every meal, no telephone booth in their sector, either, to call charitable souls who might be willing to help.

Hunger became an obsession.

All day long, damp autumn air
in my lungs, and pain, and noise, noise;
I want my supper; I've got gold
stars in my black purse!

Expecting his heart to give out at any moment, Mandelstam worked relentlessly. With the same intensity as the woodsman who chops down a tree.

Nadezhda begged him to rest, to sleep, but he refused.

He had very little time. He had to hurry.

Spring water or mud, the poems sprang forth.

Writing up to the last palpitation of the blood in his veins.

Writing while walking, walking while feeling drawn into himself for protection.

Writing indissociable from walking.

'How worn were his soles,' Nadezhda wrote in her memoirs.

Five metres from the door to the window, and back from the window to the door, one hundred times, a thousand times as if his feet were tied to a giant reel in hell.

Nadezhda would make copies. Nadezhda hid the poems wherever she could.

Passed them along.

On his neighbours, deported like he, Mandelstam gave reports to the NKVD. He was a snitch.

How is it possible that a poem that hasn't even been published deserves exile.

All we hear is the Kremlin mountaineer
the murderer and peasant-slayer

Those verses circulated from mouth to mouth. Approved or not, their author would pay for them with his life.

His mental troubles began at that time.

Nightmares and hallucinations had one subject: Stalin.

Stalin is looking for his glasses under Mandelstam's moth-eaten blanket. Finds them, places them on his nose and asks him to see him in his reality, but Mandelstam sees only the void.

Stalin doesn't exist. Stalin is a figment of his imagination, he decides.

Should he forbid himself from sleeping, to escape him?

'Guess who was sitting on this chair before you?' the barber asks him in a dream.

Seeing that he didn't answer, the barber hands him a mirror.

The face he sees isn't his own, it is Stalin's.

A face without a body, it floats in the air, runs after Mandelstam who speeds away as fast as he can.

The more he runs, the more faded the face becomes, until only the moustache remains, like two fangs, two cockroaches.

Huge cockroach-whiskers laughing,

. . .

Whenever he's got a victim, he glows like a
    broad-chested
Georgian munching a raspberry

—Mandelstam wrote in 1933.

'Mandelstam is lucky to be exiled, he deserves to be shot,' said Madame Pasternak who never tolerated her husband's empathy for the poet.

'Zina baked a cake, I'll bring you a piece,' says Pasternak to Mandelstam who is paying him a visit during a brief stay in Leningrad.

Returns from the kitchen with empty hands. Zina refuses to part with a slice of cake for Mandelstam, refuses to come say hello, demands that he leave her house.

Pasternak accompanies him to the train station, lets several trains pass before leaving him. He continues to feel great guilt. Mandelstam doesn't hold it against his friend who is known for his submission to his wife and to the regime. The three hundred roubles he slips into his pocket before the doors close, it will pay the rent of the poet who is forbidden from working.

'Who is that Mandelstam who doesn't think of anyone, and yet demands that we provide him a place to live, and work,' Tikhonov would say in front of witnesses.

Nadezhda's reaction, thirty years later:

> From his point of view, Tikhonov was quite right. In the eyes of someone so totally devoted to the regime M. was an anomaly, a harmful emanation of the past, a person for

whom there was no room in a literature where
positions were allotted by higher authority.

Voronezh: An enchanting landscape four months out of twelve—sleet, slush, mud.

Hunger the rest of the year.

Voronezh glorified cruelty.

Boasting the largest number of deported criminals in the time of Peter the Great brought great pride to the inhabitants.

Assassin Street, Passage of Thieves, Impasse of Embezzlers from the State, Avenue of Counterfeiters—the streets and avenues of Voronezh carried the names of their crimes.

A secret agent disguised as a deportee, the neighbour in the room next to the Mandelstams' catches mice, grills them on the gas heater and eats them.

The mouse held by its tail above the flame: his weekly performance. The terrorized squealing of the tortured animal accompanied by the monstrous laugh of the ogre.

The vital minimum: bread, tea and cigarettes, are lacking when Nadezhda can't find translation work.

At night, hunger pushes them into the icy streets.

Looking at the plates of the diners through restaurant windows makes them salivate.

'Do you know what's in the plate of the man sitting in the middle? What is that orange colour?'

'An orange.'

'You mean an orange peel.'

'And the woman with large, white breasts that touch the tablecloth—do you know what she's eating?'

'—snow. You have it under your feet.'

Hunger in Voronezh more tenacious than the snow trampled by the desperate couple.

Blinded by the whirling snow, they go home sensing they were bringing the road with them.

Not the slightest generosity or goodness in the inhabitants of Voronezh, just denunciations, searches.

Everyone is a snitch.

Five moves in three years.

'Why must I wander my entire life?' wondered the one who dreamt of a true lodging with a window looking out over a street, while Nadezhda dreamt of a pantry filled with vegetables, cheese and milk.

'Let's get a cow,' she suggested one morning.

'A cow needs hay. Hay costs money. And where would we put it?'

Nadezhda's dejected look around the room.

'So let's get a chicken, instead. There's room under the bed. You could eat as many eggs as you wanted.'

No cow, no chicken, hunger for the Mandelstams was a vocation.

They were always waiting for something, a call, a letter, money, but nothing arrived.

Snow, as far as the eye could see, blocked the horizon.

His requests to go to Moscow to take care of his literary affairs were refused.

'Not having published for years, you don't have any literary affairs,' they told him.

Which explained those comings and goings during the day to beg a few roubles from the Writers' Union, mainly from Shklovsky who deprived himself in order to come to their aid.

The generous Shklovsky fed the couple and slipped a few roubles into Mandelstam's pocket each time they met.

Returning to Voronezh on the last train, the couple argued.

Would they be able to afford a cart at the station?

Useless arguments, the carts were snatched up by travellers more alert than they, they always went home on foot into their glacial room, fifteen square metres divided into three areas by a curtain and an armoire.

At night, Mandelstam ran to a shop that printed his poems.

Poems exchanged for bread, cigarettes, and sometimes a bottle of Ukrainian wine.

The bag of supplies in his arm thrilled Nadezhda.

Not a single collection of poems published in twenty years.

He compensates for this by writing countless letters to anyone in a position of authority at the Writers' Union.

Mandelstam writes to Bukharin, to Stavsky, to Surkov, to Fadeiev, even to Marshak who doesn't like his poetry, writes to his friends and his enemies. He is hungry, cold, afraid.

His distress calls worry his friends: Akhmatova and Pasternak intervene so he will be transferred to another city and together give him five hundred roubles, when the seventy roubles Akhmatova receives every month for her retirement are scarcely enough to pay for her cigarettes.

Akhmatova advises him to go on vacation in the country, to Zadonsk, to get out of Voronezh to write when she herself no longer dares to.

Her silence guarantees the life of her son Lev.

She has burnt all her poems since he went to prison.

She is sometimes able to recite, her eyes closed, a verse or two. But forgets the rest. It's visible on her lips that move without a sound.

The voice of Akhmatova, his friend, his accomplice, is superimposed on his.

Her voice makes the poem, he said.

They led you away at dawn,
I followed you, like a mourner.
In the dark front room the children were crying.

'Akhmatova's poetry is liturgical, the only language you can hold up to destiny when it becomes tragic,' wrote Nicolas Bouvier.

With the five hundred roubles in his pocket, Mandelstam and Nadezhda leave Voronezh for the countryside.

Their landlady raises chickens, has an orchard.

They eat all they want, walk in the fields. Mandelstam gives a goldfinch to their landlady's son. Watches the cat walk around the cage, gives the dog a sugar cube.

The goldfinch's singing chased away his sadness.

The dog taught him to play.

The cat to observe.

What luxury in this hamlet of misery
The melodious mane of water

Nadezhda envies the woman who lives far from the snitches and the crusher of men.

Their landlady fixes them delicious meals but Mandelstam hardly touches them.

The spasms of his diseased heart never leave him in peace.

He is choking; suffocates at times.

The poet suffocates from not being published.

His poem on Stalin shuts all doors to him

All we hear is the Kremlin mountaineer
the murderer and peasant-slayer

followed by even more virulent lines:

An idol is idle, inside a mountain,
. . .
A hypnotized bone, tied in a knot . . .

The poem, his only weapon against the tyrant who labours to reduce him to crumbs.

They leave the countryside with heavy hearts.

The cat ate the goldfinch before disappearing.

Mandelstam longs for nature.

He would like to be the brother of an oak tree that confronts winter without losing its leaves, a robust tree that creates the frames of houses that stand up to the weather.

His wish would be granted twenty-six years later by another Jewish poet with a destiny as painful as his, Paul Celan, who dedicated to Mandelstam his collection *Die Niemandsrose*, and this poem:

> *The silver coin melts on your tongue,*
> *tasting like tomorrow, like for ever, a road*
> *to Russia climbs into your heart,*
> *where the Karelian birch*
> *has been*
> *waiting, where*
> *the name Osip approaches you, you tell him*
> *something he knows already, he takes it, relieves*
>   *you of it with both hands,*
> *you take off his arm at the shoulder, right arm,*
>   *left arm,*
> *you put your own arms in their place, along with*
>   *hands, fingers, palm lines,*
> *—what was torn off is rejoined—*
> *you've got both, so take them, have them:*
> *the name, the name, the hand, the hand,*
> *take them as a pledge, then,*
> *and he does the same and you both*
> *have what is yours and what was his*

Return to Voronezh on 1 May, the entire city is celebrating Workers' Day. Flags are flying in the sky.

Marxist songs teeming with emotion.

But Mandelstam's heart isn't there.

He feels hunted.

The walls separating the rooms in the communal flats have ears.

His neighbours are spying on him.

The vise tightens.

Mandelstam, who knows, takes refuge in the past.

He thinks fondly of mainland Russia, of its izbas, its peasants, its horses, its bulbous steeples. He also remembers his childhood holidays with his parents in a village in Finland.

All the women are laundresses
all the men senators
you can win a cow in the lottery

His only moments of happiness are found in his travels abroad: Italy, Germany, Finland, Armenia with its orange-stone buildings where he stayed for some time with Nadezhda:

> *I drank a toast in spirit to the health of young Armenia, with its houses of orange stone, to its white-toothed commissars, to its horse sweat and its restless stomp of waiting lines: and to its mighty language which we are unworthy to speak and of which, in our incompetence, we can only steer clear.*

—he wrote fifteen years earlier in *Journey to Armenia*.

The photos of Stalin on the walls in Voronezh give Mandelstam goosebumps.

His moustache, his lips painted blood red. Those of a predator.

An enraptured city. Blaring music.

The sound of boots, cymbals, drums encircle the poet from all directions, compressing him.

Convoys pass by.

Ovations to the Father of the People burst in the air.

Flags struck with the hammer and sickle fill the space.

The din and praise roll around in the poet's head.

Mandelstam faints.

Mandelstam collapses on the pavement.

In the hospital, he calls Stalin's moustache cockroaches and in the confusion writes to the Writers' Union to complain:

'Spare me this humiliation. What I endure in Voronezh has no name.'

His friends reproach him for beating a path straight to the execution pole. But he doesn't care. Mayakovsky did the same thing.

Mayakovsky announced his suicide in one of his poems.

Mandelstam is committing suicide.

Looking out the window in his hospital room, he must think he's a bird opening his arms and jumping into the void.

Nadezhda arrives and seizes him by his coat.

An empty coat, that's all that she has left in her hands.

Caught one floor down.

He suffers contusions. But it is she, his young, twenty-nine-year-old wife, who is ill. Her nerves have frayed.

She goes to Moscow for treatment and there, by miracle, she is able to keep her room on Furmanov Street.

Her mother, Vera, comes from Kiev, will take her place with Mandelstam.

Learning of the suicide attempt, Pasternak intervenes with Stalin so the poet will be pardoned.

Stalin calls Pasternak to reassure him.

The absolute monarch addresses the fate of the ruined poet. The affair is made known. Stalin emerges from it all the greater but there is no miracle.

Mandelstam remains an undesirable in Moscow.

And Pasternak did what he could.

Pasternak and Mandelstam, such contrast in the lives they chose.

Pasternak allowed himself to be tamed by power.

Mandelstam, a nomad, a rebel, confronts power.

Mandelstam flees friendship.

Pasternak seeks it even if he dared publish *Doctor Zhivago* abroad.

Nadezhda Mandelstam, wed to her husband's poems.

Zina Pasternak who despises the poet tears up Mandelstam's letters to her husband.

'You're lucky to be in exile and not shot,' she tells him again when they meet.

Intellectuals were shot with a vengeance in the winter of 1937.

Arrests always took place at 6 p.m.

A time Mandelstam dreaded.

He became febrile, suffocated.

All footsteps caused him to panic.

In the street he felt followed, changed his route, hid behind courtyard doors.

A neighbour advised Nadezhda to move her clock up.

Which she did.

Seeing it was 7 p.m., he could breathe easy.

Arrests, body and flat searches were often followed by theft.

The neighbours divided up the spoils belonging to the one who had just been arrested.

> The usual reaction to each new arrest was that some retreated even further into their shells (which, incidentally, never saved them) while others responded with a chorus of jeers for the victim . . .

—wrote Nadezhda in her memoirs.

In the beginning, people came running from all directions, no one wanted to miss the show.

But then it became repetitive, people got tired, stopped paying attention. The family of the person arrested didn't react.

Deported or shot, they would find out one day. The NKVD let people know.

Searches, arrests, executions brought 700,000 deaths in one year. The famine organized by Stalin would kill just as many.

> . . . *this hard-living people—*
> *giving birth, sleeping,*
> *screaming, nailed to the earth.*

—wrote Mandelstam in those days.

In her memoirs, Nadezhda speaks of her visit to a family living in a village near Saviolovo. Some friends had taken her there.

Framed photos of four who had been executed were lined up on the same wall.

In a similar frame, a three-year-old child, longish hair, was smiling at the camera.

'Who is the child?'

'The brother of those shot.'

'What happened to him?'

They move their lips.

'Put in an orphanage twenty years ago, he ended up becoming a policeman. Now he arrests people.'

Curled up under his blanket in the transit camp.

So close to death, Mandelstam continues to hope for a letter from Romain Rolland who promised Pasternak we would intervene with Stalin on his behalf.

Pasternak always helped him unbeknownst to his wife, Zina, who always asked him the same question every time she saw him:

'Are you still writing those little things?'

Wedded to her comfort, Pasternak's wife declared that her children loved Stalin best. Pasternak and she came after.

Stupid but pretentious, speaking about Mandelstam's poem on Stalin, she said:

'A Jew born in Poland shouldn't have said that . . . '

The Jew of Polish origin, celebrated at the age of twenty before being betrayed by his peers, bouncing from exile to exile, forgotten during his lifetime, would be recognized after his death with the help of other poets.

Paul Celan would translate him into German.

Joseph Brodsky would translate him into English.

And especially with the help of his wife Nadezhda who would publish his works thirty years after his death.

It took a political change, the arrival of Khrouchtchev, for Nadezhda to be able to publish her husband's poems, he who didn't want to leave the world without testifying to what had gone on before his eyes.

He wrote day and night, in hospitals, in prison, in the street by the light of the streetlamps, wrote on an empty stomach, surrounded by snitches.

With three years of not writing due to a sort of numbness.

Only Party poets who ate from the hand of the regime published their works at that time.

His own hand transformed into stone, he no longer dared to write; he learnt his poems by heart, dictated them to Nadezhda who copied them and distributed them to the few friends who agreed to keep them.

A letter from Mandelstam among his papers aggravated the case of the powerful Bukharin, accused of plotting against the State.

Executed like a mere plotter whereas he had served the dictator.

Lucky were those who left a body behind them. So many people disappeared.

Where did they end up?

'We rarely attended a burial,' Nadezhda wrote.

Disappeared from one day to the next.

No coffin, no shroud, no name on a gravestone.

No widows or orphans, either.

The husband deported, the wife was considered divorced and could remarry.

To save their skin, the children disavowed their father, slandered him.

Horrific scenes, Mandelstam covered his ears to escape them.

We have a spider-work of honest old plaid—
drape it over me like a flag, when I die.

—he wrote at the time.

The Mandelstams' moth-eaten plaid blanket became the couple's true home. That is where they could memorize the poems, take turns reciting a fragment, go through all the letters of the alphabet when a verse wouldn't come to them.

It was under that blanket that they would take refuge when they heard about raids being planned.

The announcement of raids sowed panic.

Frightened people ran in all directions for fear of being arrested, avoided sleeping at home.

A clean-up operation.

Mandelstam heard the sound of boots, heard the knocking at the door.

Mandelstam continues to hear them under the blanket pierced with a hole in the transit camp.

Through that hole, the madman, the living dead man, the poet, can observe his assassins in white tunics.

The camp doctors have decided to inject him with the rabies virus. He's convinced of this.

My eyelashes sting. There's a tear sticking
to my heart. I feel what's coming, but no fear.
A storm's coming . . .

He had written those lines a year earlier, when he had the impression he was sitting on a branch so dry that it threatened at any moment to break and plunge him to the ground.

Samatikha and its Writers' Residency. That was a year ago, you might as well say a century. The old, run-down house that was meant to care for his heart turned out to be a passageway to death.

It was there that his phobias fed by an ever-growing fear began. His nights at Samatikha fed his nightmares.

He runs towards a bridge to flee the fire that is ravaging the town.

Arriving at the middle, he is unable to go any further.

The other half of the bridge has collapsed.

Nadezhda on the other side of the river holds out her hand but he can't reach her.

Besides, Nadezhda isn't Nadezhda any more.

No longer has the same name.

She begs him to change his name if he wants to survive.

To write an ode to Stalin if he wants to eat something other than chickpeas.

How can he trust her when her voice is no longer the same?

When her words are swallowed by the din of the flowing river.

Beneath his feet.

Its muddy water skims the trunks of trees, human trunks, branches and hair entwined.

The same visions return night after night.

Mandelstam has become mad without knowing it; it wasn't what he said that made him believe that, but the way in which he said it.

Nadezhda accused the food: Mandelstam lacked iron and she made him drink concoctions of rusty nails dissolved in wine.

Mandelstam, Akhmatova, Tsvetaeva and so many other muzzled poets, isolated from their young readers, deported.

Deportations often followed by executions. Gumilev, Akhmatova's husband, shot without a trial at the age of twenty-seven.

Her son Lev deported, Akhmatova didn't write any more. Her poems could potentially aggravate her son's case. You had to be invisible to survive. Pretend not to exist.

> *We live, not feeling the ground under our feet,*
> *no one hears us more than a dozen steps away,*
>
> *And when there's enough for half a small chat—*
> *ah, we remember the Kremlin mountaineer:*
>
> *Thick fingers, fat like worms, greasy . . .*

—Mandelstam would say in his poem.

Those who had some potatoes, some pork or some cabbage in their soup considered themselves fortunate. Those who got by unnoticed.

'Take off your hat, you're going to be noticed,' said Nadezhda to her husband when they were walking in the street.

Mandelstam, who liked his hat, took it off.

The worst death is that of thought, he said.

The poet spoke of that death in his poems but no one paid attention.

Mayakovsky speaking of suicide wasn't heard, either.

'All the while preparing themselves for death, people try to delay the inevitable end,' Mandelstam wrote to Pasternak, who tried to appease him.

They close their eyes, pretend to live, look for a flat, buy nice shoes, and turn away from the grave dug for them.

Intransigent, Mandelstam exasperated his friends with his requests for money and his suicide threats.

His aborted suicide attempt worried his mother-in-law. Nadezhda's mother sells all that she has in the Ukraine to join her son-in-law and daughter in Voronezh.

She wants to share their exile, watch over Mandelstam when he is released from the hospital.

To relieve Nadezhda who is tending to her nerves in Moscow.

Vera shuts her eyes to the walks her son-in-law takes with young Natasha who distracts him from his troubles.

He writes love poems to her, reads them to her then immediately destroys them. No woman in the world can replace his wife, who is still in Moscow struggling to put an end to their exile after three hellish years in Voronezh.

The romance between the banned poet and his young admirer turned into friendship after Natasha became engaged to a man of means.

Mandelstam is invited by the generous fiancé to dinner at the restaurant of a big hotel.

He reconnects with refined dishes, fine wines.

With his head thrown back he watches, dreamily, the circling clouds of smoke from his cigar.

Doesn't forget to thank his generous host who is leaving with the young girl who enflamed his senses.

Everything has an end.

He returns to his room with three oranges.

Keeps one for him, one for Nadezhda and slips the third under his sleeping mother-in-law's pillow.

A doctor for thirty years in a working-class section of Kiev, Vera notices the same phenomenon in Voronezh.

Those who are hungry become depressed and take refuge in sleep.

They get up in the morning, go to their place of work, then return home quickly to go back to bed.

The people in the street look like ghosts. They sleep to forget their hunger.

Famine everywhere, even in the countryside.

Grass scorched by a horribly hot summer, there was a lack of hay. Starving cows gave scant milk. Mules had trouble pulling carts. A common sight, horses collapsed on the road, their masters whipping them to make them stand up.

The land refused to feed people or animals.

That was when Tsvetaeva, back from France where she had been living in poverty, began to dig frozen earth looking for anything to feed her son, Mur, who mistreated her. Beat her.

The only remaining member of her family—her daughter and her husband had been deported to Siberia—she bore his beatings.

Tsvetaeva scratched the earth until the day of her death, when she was found hanging from a beam in her attic.

Her poem dedicated to Pasternak goes back to 1925.

Distance: versts, miles . . .
divide us; they've dispersed us,
to make us behave quietly
              at our different ends of the earth.

Distance: how many miles of it
lie between us now—disconnected—
crucified—then dissected.
and they don't know—it unites us.

Tsvetaeva loved Pasternak who didn't love her back.

Tsvetaeva rejected Mandelstam who loved her.

They had seen each other twenty years earlier, during the poet's stay in Moscow.

A great seductress, Tsvetaeva encouraged him during their first encounter only to leave him the next day.

Back in St Petersburg, Mandelstam forgot the woman but not her poems.

Tsvetaeva, an outspoken woman. A woman thirsting for love.

How to explain her rejection of her Russian compatriots, exiled as she was, during her years in Paris? And was it to reconnect to life that she maintained a correspondence with Pasternak that lasted several years?

Feverish letters from both sides that stopped after their one and only rendezvous in a Metro station in Leningrad.

The love that had endured as long as they were apart, lived, then stopped all of a sudden.

Disappointed by her appearance, the author of *Doctor Zhivago* leaves Tsvetaeva with a few words of excuse.

No desire at all to restore a taste for life in a woman who had prematurely aged. Become ugly.

Her parents' lavish home in Moscow transformed into communal flats, Tsvetaeva moved in with Mur into a shack in the woods, far from other houses.

It was there, in that wooden hovel where the wind blew through the cracks, that she hung herself from a beam on the ceiling.

An unexpected end for one who was born of the great bourgeoisie.

Served by an army of servants in the lavish family home, Tsvetaeva was a member of the golden youth of the time.

Her husband, Sergei Efron, and daughter were deported to Siberia.

All her horizons blocked, without the slightest ray of hope for the future, the great poetess preferred to leave the stage with a kick of the chair upon which she had climbed.

A kick to the world that had abandoned her.

Mandelstam is the only one who hears his voice recite his poems to his neighbours, deportees like he.

Poetry, the last thing the horde of prisoners who could be shot from one day to the next are interested in.

They want bread. Not words.

They are angry, the least ill among them hold up avenging fists.

Their shouts don't stop the poet from continuing his reading.

His voice, he's certain, will ultimately drown out their din.

In addition to bread, they demand soup that is less diluted and demand to be treated as human beings.

Crammed together for months in the transit camp located a stone's throw from Vladivostok, without seeing the sky.

Without seeing the end of the tunnel, without knowing the date of their departure for Siberia which has become the promised land compared to the hell of the camp.

No train to take them to Siberia, they're told.

The rumours in the chaos take the place of decrees.

From all the cities throughout the country, train carriages discharge onto the platforms the cargo of men to be deported or shot, then go off looking for more offenders, other dissidents to deport or shoot.

How do they choose?

Who decides to shorten or to prolong a life?

'Skim the country, rid it of all those who think differently from the regime,' are the marching orders.

The sound of boots interrupts Mandelstam's sleep, though no one is walking; typhus has nailed his bunk-mates to their planks.

'Get up, you're forbidden to stay in the camp. Forbidden to die without Stalin's permission.'

A mirage, hands that shake him, the mouth shouting his name.

It doesn't matter to Mandelstam if he has lost his mind, he knows he is a poet and that's enough for him.

He also knows he's still alive, otherwise he wouldn't know that his bunkmates are called Fedor, Piotr, Vlada or Anton.

He knows their names but can't connect a face to each of those names.

Names, his lifesaver. He clings to them so he won't sink. He would die if he ever forgot them.

Anton threatens to commit suicide every morning then changes his mind once he has swallowed Mandelstam's bit of bread after his own.

Piotr announces the end of the world every daybreak.

Fedor won't die as long as Stalin is alive. Surviving him will enable him one day to spit on his face, on his coffin.

Whether workers, intellectuals or peasants, they all harbour the same hatred for the tyrant who has destroyed three generations.

Only Vlada, seventeen years old, is optimistic.

He will survive thanks to his fiancée who is a laundress in the army.

Her supplications slipped into the ironed jacket pockets of an officer will end up drawing attention to his case.

Freed, he will get married, have children, write books at home. He will never go out, and will remain among his words.

Having become wealthy from the sale of his books, he will construct with his own hands a house without windows, without doors, without any orifice.

Vlada gets very excited as he talks.

Being an epileptic, it's in his interest to calm down.

The Vladivostok transit camp, a passage to madness.

To the question: 'What are you writing now?' asked by a Party poet, Mandelstam responded,

'I'm writing about an imprisoned Jewish poet, one sonnet a day, then I learn it by heart. When I'm free, I will transcribe it and will return to prison.'

You have conquered it all, no yoke stops you.
Every obstacle is dead under your blows.
Now you have climbed to the heights.
Be ready to bend under your jealous duties.
Benefactors, you owe a great reckoning to us.
You must still contain others and you;
you must know how to come down

—André Chénier once wrote.

Mandelstam is sure he is still alive.

Dead, he wouldn't hear the clicking of his neighbours' jaws. Chewed for a long time, the same mouthful of bread fools hunger.

A bit of bread in the morning, soup in the evening: the only events of the day, whereas the evacuation of a dead body from a neighbouring plank is hardly noticed.

Indifferent to anything concerning their survival, but so attentive to the sound of the shovels that interrupt their sleep.

Are they digging the dirt on the other side of the wall for them? A different sound made by the body dragged on the wet ground after a rain and for the one tossed into a grave. They learnt to differentiate them, learnt to distinguish the sick man who still had one or two days of life in him from the one who has only a few hours.

Only the mad poet hidden under his blanket escapes their prognostics. Dead on the outside, he continues to mutter things. His words refuse to die. His arm, too, raised by his neighbour, who takes advantage of his ration of bread.

The typhus that doesn't distinguish between young and old still doesn't empty all the planks.

New invalids immediately occupy them.

As if illness has affected all the inhabitants of Russia.

As if they will all be exiled one day or another to Siberia.

All shot.

The image of a cemetery at the edge of the village of Zadonsk comes to Mandelstam, so close to death.

The sweetness of the air around the ageing unkempt tombstones.

The bone-coloured rectangles shimmer in the autumn sun.

The dominant note, the blood of the elderberry vine on the wall of the empty church that is crumbling to ruin.

Through the overgrown vegetation, a crucified one continued to drip his blood on the moss-covered marble of what once was an altar.

Absent icons, dark spots on the walls tell of their former existence, no benches, either. Those in good shape are repurposed in youth centres, the worn-out ones become logs for a fireplace.

The fatherland: the only God.

Nadezhda and Mandelstam were strolling along that day.

The columns with crucifixes at the top had stopped them in their tracks.

Forgetting she was Jewish, Nadezhda made the sign of the cross.

Mandelstam took off his hat:

'Hello, dead people,' he cried joyfully.

The dead in the cemetery of Zadonsk smelt like wilted flowers and trampled grass whereas his transit-camp neighbours smelt like sweat, vomit and diarrhoea.

Half of those who arrive in the camp will die within a week.

Convoys continue endlessly to arrive at the little train station. The carriages spill out their contents before setting off for other cities where other offenders await them, others accused of conspiring against the State.

A stench of rot and smoke.

Nadezhda doesn't care.

She is looking for Mandelstam in the crowd of the deported.

Looks for his face through the windows of the dark soot-covered carriages.

Looks for a letter that her husband might have thrown out for her while the train was passing through the station.

She reads all the papers lying on the tracks.

Every piece of writing is studied, deciphered. But none is addressed to her.

A woman lets her sleep in her shack in the country-side.

In the morning, she runs once more to the station and watches all the trains that pass during the day.

She goes back to her landlady at night. With heavy steps, a heavy heart.

The bay leaves gathered on her way home pay for her bowl of soup.

All the railroad workers know the wife of the deported poet.

Watch her search all the carriages with her eyes. Strike the burning metal with her palms. Banging her fist on the doors, wrenching their hearts.

They hold back their tears when Mandelstam's name travels through the smoke.

Nadezhda's shout is louder than the sound of the train's whistle.

'Open up, let the poet Mandelstam get out,' she begs while the poet is dying, semi-conscious, a stone's throw away from the station.

But Nadezhda doesn't know.

Armed with the sense of smell of a hunting dog, Nadezhda would have detected the presence of her husband from his blanket.

But Nadezhda is not a dog but a woman in love.

The wife of Osip Mandelstam.

Once a handsome man.

Now a worn-down old man.

A frightened old man under his blanket, with his hallucinations and delirium.

The voices of his neighbours reach his ears through the tattered screen of the fabric.

He catches one out of two of the words they speak.

How difficult it is to put the words together in a sentence.

To give meaning to what seems to be important to them.

Listening to them, they have nothing to regret.

Conscience as white as the snow of the Urals but they found themselves in the wrong place, at the mercy of raids.

Should have moved before, left no trace behind.

No telephone or electricity, no children registered at birth, no schooling, no hospitalizations.

No death certificate.

To fade away. If needed, penetrate underground. Dig one's own lair. Imitate the hare, the ant, the weasel . . .

Wild imaginings flourish in the camp where the dead and the living are piled up like sardines.

Everyone shares his story. The others need not necessarily believe it.

Fedor's mother made him wash the feet of her Czech father-in-law and drink the water afterward to thank him for supplying their daily bread.

Anton who worked for a ditch-digger had good reason to throw his employer, a tyrant, into the pit he had just dug and cover him with dirt until his final cry died out.

He had forced him to eat dirt before each burial.

Vlada's case was more serious than those of his comrades.

While walking in the fields he dared to pick an apple that was hanging over the fence of a dacha.

The noise he made alerted the owner of the property. A high functionary of the NKVD.

During his interrogation, his theft became an intrusion onto private property in an attempt to spy.

Should they believe Piotr who turned Stalin into the cause of all his misfortune?

'He stole my wife.'

Uncomfortable looks from the others.

'I mean it's because of Stalin that my wife left me,' he specified after clearing his throat. 'Dying from hunger, Katyusha left me for the stock boy of the local cooperative.'

Four cases connected by the same motivation: hunger.

To eat: the final thought of the Soviet citizen tied to the execution pole, thinks the poet under his blanket who refuses to eat, and without hesitation allows himself to perish.

Difficult to know if Fedor, Piotr, Vlada and Anton have told their own story or that of someone else.

To put yourself in someone else's skin is a recreation.

Making things up is not forbidden in the Vladivostok camp.

Each person indulges his overactive imagination.

No one doubts what Anton says, that the dead of his village rise up at each first quarter moon to walk around the places they inhabited before returning to their graves.

To the question: 'Where is your village?' Anton scratches his head until it bleeds, and finally extracts a louse.

Throws it on the ground.

Then stomps on it, enraged, crushing it.

He has forgotten. A name that begins with the letter F. It's on the tip of his tongue.

The clouds of words from Piotr, Fedor, Vlada and Anton become drops of water on Mandelstam's face. The dead man is listening.

The dead man sweats. A dead man who listens and sweats is alive.

The transit camp for Siberia hums with rumours.

'There is life after death,' proclaims a believer.

Only Mandelstam doubts. He would consider himself alive the day when he writes a new poem, when Stalin stops showing up in his dreams.

He saw him pass by yesterday, leading a procession several kilometres long:

Those who were shot, those dead during deportation.

They were walking in step.

The ground pounded by their steps cracked open as after an earthquake.

Seated on a wall overlooking the scene, Mandelstam counted them on his fingers, lamenting the fact that he had only ten.

Arriving where he was sitting, they all bowed before setting off at a good pace.

The same age, the same face, the same size, they seemed to be the same man multiplied to infinity.

They marched along in perfect order before disappearing over the horizon.

Leaving in their wake pages covered with his writing.

Which rustled in the wind ready to fly away.

His poems kept by his secret readers surged out of their hiding places.

The sound of the paper resembled applause.

It didn't matter if those who were keeping them were shot or deported.

Since they would be reborn on the other side of the planet.

The last man disappeared, a voice rang out:

It's for you, Mandelstam, that I arranged this
    procession
for you that I've sacrificed all these men
You can thank me now that the survival of your
    work is ensured
Without me you would be one poet among others;
your poems: traces of ink on a page.

Recognizable among all the others, Stalin's voice continued to thunder in Mandelstam's ears, the poet balancing between wakefulness and sleep.

'Music comforts a man.'

A strange statement from the mouth of a brute like Fedor.

The order to play something cheerful is met with laughter.

No instruments in sight, only wooden planks piled up to the ceiling.

'Play what you know,' he orders Vlada who is ready to obey him.

Vlada's fingers drum on his lips imitating a harmonica.

His breath is transformed into sounds, notes, melody, a mazurka.

Caught up in his own playing, Vlada becomes animated, ebullient.

His feet tap out the rhythm.

His cheeks swollen with air, feed the sounds.

The boy has a forge in his throat.

The order to stop the noise stops the notes in the musician's mouth.

The guard named Taras Bulba doesn't like music, doesn't like Vlada, the only one who is enduring his hell.

Sure that the love of his laundress will save him.

Taras Bulba has some news for him.

'Your fiancée has gotten married; she got tired of waiting. Understandable at her age. And no more noise.'

'Noise, yourself.'

The voice comes from under the moth-eaten blanket.

The living dead man has his word to say. No one can stop him.

The living dead man happens to think of his old father.

Of the affluent leather merchant from before the revolution, who became poor over the years.

Ill and unable to be taken in by any of his children. He risks finding himself on the street when he gets out of the hospital.

Mandelstam sees in his thoughts the letter he wrote to him six months earlier, after he had just left Voronezh.

Mandelstam begged his father to be patient.

Back from his exile, he had lots of plans. Everything seemed to be smiling on him. With his poems published, he would be celebrated by his peers and his father would be able to come and live with him. The royalties he earned would easily pay for the dacha with its garden that Nadezhda dreamt of. 'You will have your room, my brother Shura will have his. Nadezhda's sister will join us. It is time for the family to once again be united under the same roof.'

The letter is dated 15 May 1938.

Mandelstam didn't want to lower his arms. Wanted always to believe in better days to come.

Dead, he kept his arms stretched above, a camp survivor would tell Nadezhda.

The frozen earth in that month of December and the skin of their hands sticking to the shovels, the ditch-diggers left him on the ground for an entire day before they could bury him.

The wind blew at his patriarch's beard.

His face was completely serene.

How did Vlada climb on the roof of the barracks without any of the guards stopping him?

Too light to hang himself, he decided to die of the cold.

Sitting on the chimney as on a throne, he proclaims that there is no life for him after Katyinka. His trousers, his shirt, his shapka distributed among his comrades, he keeps his underpants.

Modesty requires it.

'Come down from there, Vlada, you're going to catch your death,' shouts one of his heirs, but he doesn't blink.

An entire morning spent begging him. But Vlada seems frozen on the chimney.

The night falls, and Vlada is still perched on the roof.

Mandelstam, who hasn't moved in three days, begins to stir.

'Get down from there you little brat,' he murmurs from under his moth-eaten blanket.

And Vlada comes down.

Deep in a coma, Mandelstam continues to exert a power over his comrades.

Down from his perch, Vlada thanks the poet for his advice, kisses his hand, then lies down.

He has decided to sleep until the last day of his life.

The noise from the trains doesn't keep the dying poet from reciting his poems to himself, from proclaiming them.

He hears ovations. He can die in peace now that he knows he's appreciated.

Less mad, Mandelstam would understand that what he takes for ovations are only requests—his friends want bread, not words.

Poetry is superfluous when the stomach is empty and bodies are thrown into a common grave the way a baker puts his bread in the oven.

The dead—the daily bread of the transit camp of Vladivostok.

The name is never mentioned. The numbered tag affixed to the body's foot marks its identity.

Nadezhda looks for Mandelstam at the train station, the obligatory stop en route to Siberia.

Days and days walking up and down the platforms, scratching on the ground with her gaze, looking for a word scratched on a bit of paper, telling her the place where he is and if he is still alive.

Deportees wanting to get news to their family resort to that process. Arrests are so abrupt. People disappear. The families are not always told.

Returning from exile after a few years, there have been men looking for their wives, their children. Some cried.

Overwhelmed, overcome by their begging, the functionaries meant to inform them slam down their windows.

Potential witnesses, members of a deportee's family were often killed. Denouncing one's father or mother was the only way to stay alive.

People were heard thanking Stalin for having rid them of the bad patriot that their father had been. Their denunciation shouted out in the streets.

Mandelstam saw one proclaim his hatred for his father while sobbing.

A strange era, spoken words rarely connected to thoughts. Denunciations were common currency in cities, the countryside, even in Voronezh where every-one knew everyone else. People of good faith spoke of misunderstandings.

The end of their exile in Voronezh and their return to Moscow, yet another misunderstanding. They believed they had earned the right to a normal life.

A parenthesis, the few days of respite in their flat on Furmanov Street.

The doctor and the two officers who arrived at their flat one morning only wanted what was best for Mandelstam.

An arrest disguised as concern for his health.

He was going to benefit from care he would receive at a Writers' Residency, located 150 kilometres from Moscow.

End of the line, they told themselves.

So it would be possible to go back and forth in one day.

A name came back to him while they were loading him into the van.

Why had he agreed to go to Samatikha? wondered Mandelstam in a burst of clarity. Writers' Residency. A trap.

Why had he agreed to go to Samatikha?

Mandelstam has become a ball in the hands of the NKVD, in those of the leaders of the Writers' Union, too.

Lies, their wishes for a quick recovery the day before he left.

Lies, their farewells with a tear in their eye when they had planned his deportation and his execution.

His sentence of five years in prison for deeds against the revolution, was not revealed the day of his arrest.

Nadezhda would learn of it later and would rack her memory seeking the slightest omission, sin or misdeed.

'They no longer knew what to do with me. My worn-out shoes, my patriarch's beard, my worn-out cane weighed on their conscience.' He had fewer and fewer friends. Explaining his response to Pasternak who wrote to him after the heart attack that felled him one day in front of the theatre:

'Thank you for remembering me and for allowing me to hear your voice. It is more precious to me than any true help.

'I continue to weaken and I have trouble leaving my room. I owe my second life to my single and inestimable friend, my wife.

'However my illness may develop, I would like to retain my clarity which is sometimes murky and that frightens me. My forced stay in Voronezh has proven fatal. One of the thoughts that tortures me most is that I will never see you. Don't you plan to come visit me? It seems that it is the only important thing you could do for me.'

A stone having rolled down from the mountain
lay in the valley,
torn loose of its own accord
or thrown down by a sentient hand . . .

Weeks pacing up and down at the Samatikha station without having found her husband. Back in Moscow with the mad hope of seeing him in their flat, she discovers the package that she had sent him a week earlier with the note: 'Return to sender. Recipient deceased.'

The package was dated 27 December 1938.

And yet the future had seemed less dark a few months earlier when they learnt of the end of their exile in Voronezh.

Hearing the news, their neighbour, the griller of mice, threw the few things they possessed onto the pavement.

Mattress, pots, used pillows, sold for a few roubles, they took the train to Moscow, work was awaiting them in the capital. They were sure of it. Mandelstam was going to be published. Mandelstam would give a reading of his poems at the Writers' Union.

When they arrived at the station, they ran to Furmanov Street.

Their flat occupied for three years by another writer awaited them.

Each thing in its place. They would be able to live again now that their exile had come to an end.

Sure to be welcomed with open arms by his fellow poets, Mandelstam knocks on Bukharin's door, he had been so generous with him in the past, then on all doors. No one is free to see him.

Responsible for subventions, Gorky sees him. As the clothes he is wearing are worn, he gives him a shirt and a pair of trousers, then, after some thought, decides against the trousers.

Will he have to stroll around the streets of Moscow in his underwear?

Old friends who meet the couple in the stairway pretend not to recognize them or greet them grudgingly.

They have become strangers to others, strangers to themselves.

Mandelstam wants money, wants a work permit to be able to earn his living and that of his wife, wants, above all, to read his poems at the Writers' Union, insists on it. Returns to the forefront. Nadezhda, who has made the rounds of his loyal readers, has collected a good number of his poems.

The poetry reading granted, four people attend. A slap in the face of the poet, who is rejected by his peers, looking like a beggar since his return from exile. A beggar from being forced to frequent thieves and criminals.

Did he read them his poems?

Did they applaud him?

And did he think he was on a theatre stage?

Mandelstam's eyes tear up with emotion when he thinks of the huge fellow who relieved him from stone-transport duty.

To thank him, the poet recites verses from *Stone*, his first publication.

Out of print, it was republished decades later by a foreign publisher in a collection that included the poem *Tristia*.

Forced labour being incompatible with his sick heart, Mandelstam spent his days dreaming about his return to Moscow.

The city that attracted him like a magnet.

Moscow, which had replaced God in his thoughts.

I could not feel your image
in the fog, your shaky, painful image.
'Lord!'—I said
by mistake.

And like a huge bird
God's name flew out of my breast.
A thick fog swirls in front of me,
and behind me there's an empty cage.

Born a Jew, having become a Christian out of rebellion against the established order, Mandelstam went from chaos to chaos.

Back in Moscow after three years of exile in Voronezh, Mandelstam and Nadezhda felt terrible in their worn-out clothing, the same clothes they had been wearing for three years, standing in front of the marble stairs of the Writers' Union.

The same coat and hard leather boots made from Nadezhda's mother's trunk, the same coat for him, same dress for her.

The tempting smells of food being cooked stopped them at each landing.

Seated in a corner of the cafeteria, they watched the diners eat. The big pieces of meat in the plates of writers approved by the regime made them drool.

Stavsky wouldn't see him. Nor would Svorski. Bukharin wasn't there.

Humiliated, exhausted, Mandelstam collapsed on the stairs.

Resuscitated, taken home in an ambulance, he sets off again the next day.

An early start at the Literary Foundation.

Someone would have to give him a work permit, if only so he could pay his rent.

'Having been convicted, you are banned from working in Moscow. And also banned from living here,' is the response.

Stunned, Mandelstam explains that he had been told he could settle down wherever he wanted since he had served his sentence.

' —wherever you want, but outside a radius of 150 kilometres from Moscow.'

Should we return to Voronezh? he wonders in a fog before losing consciousness the second time.

The trap closes in on him. He has been freed only to be better contained, better watched.

To capture him again at the right moment.

A charitable soul advises him to be modest, to work as a guard or attendant in a cloakroom, and why not as a gardener, although he is incapable of holding a shovel; half of his heart is stricken with asthenia, he suffocates at the slightest effort.

The second heart attack in two days on the pavement in front of the Literary Foundation.

Nadezhda finds him in the hospital, his arms open in front of the open window, ready to throw himself into the void. Nadezhda was obsessed by that scene.

His botched suicide attempt delays his expulsion. He won't be deported as long as he's bedridden.

In a great show of human kindness, the police allow him a few days' rest.

Hospitalized for his heart, he is now in the hands of psychiatrists and neurologists.

Mandelstam speaks incoherently, talks about a basket that had been stolen from him twenty years ago. All the letters from his mother and his poems from that time vanished all at once. He wants his basket.

He slowly slips into madness, and Nadezhda watches helplessly the deterioration of his wonderful mind. Fear, hunger, the determination to destroy him have the final word.

Due to his accusations, Mandelstam's home is searched again.

The papers confiscated during a search of their room are in Nadezhda's writing:

'Sugar, tea flour, salt, soap, screwdriver, kill the rats . . . ink.'

The word 'ink' was suspicious. Why ink for someone who didn't write any more? They search the mattress, the pillow, inside the shoes, the bottom of the two pots.

Nadezhda clings to daily routines to forget that her great man is stricken with paranoia.

One morning, while shaving, looking into the mirror nailed above the sink, Mandelstam freezes, calls to her so she can see with her own eyes the persecution he must endure. Stalin's face is superimposed onto his each time he tries to look in the mirror.

Mandelstam embraces his hallucinations. It's useless to contradict him since he sees with his own eyes the grizzled face of the tyrant, his bushy eyebrows, his moustache, above all, the moustache, that of a walrus which he draws with a bit of coal on the polished surface of the mirror.

He never shaved again. The beard that grew year after year made him look like a hermit, a prophet.

'Father Christmas,' a child shouted when he passed him on the street.

Forbidden from living in Moscow, Mandelstam, when he gets out of the hospital, much choose another place of exile.

With the help of a few friends, the couple reviews the cities and towns located 150 kilometres from the capital.

Their flat is given to others, they are once again homeless, go from house to house.

With their own tiny housing, their friends are unable to lodge them.

A poet refuses him harshly: he accompanies Mandelstam to the building's exit admitting he never liked his poetry.

Did they spend their last night in Moscow on the street? No one knows.

I imagine them huddled together on a bench, dreamily watching the smoke from chimneys rise up in the sky.

The cold that seeps out of the ground clutches their clothes, the stars shiver, a comet suddenly extinguishes, but they don't make the sign of the cross.

'The earth is dead but it doesn't know yet. It continues to turn,' says Mandelstam.

I also imagine a dialogue between Stavsky and Surkov who were most active in making sure that Mandelstam would be expelled from Moscow while assuring him of their support.

'Nadezhda asked me for money again. I did everything I could in the past. Always begging. She really believes that nothing should prevent her husband from being published now that his exile has come to an end.'

'That woman is a manipulator. Always asking for something. Those two are never satisfied. A cursed couple. They have exhausted their friends. Eating at some of their homes, sleeping at others.'

'Mandelstam would do well to die. He's like a chicken with its head cut off, still running around.'

'Stubborn, like all Jews. He ran into the mouth of the wolf by coming back to Moscow.'

'He would have done better to stay in Voronezh with the other deportees.'

'All his friends tried to dissuade him but he never listens to anyone.'

'His ode to Stalin was a very bad idea.'

'To glorify the one he had called an executioner did not expunge his crime. He said he wrote that poem with a rope around his neck.'

'Akhmatova, who did the same, had an excuse: they were tightening the rope around her son's neck.'

'He botched his suicide, another bad idea.'

'It didn't earn him any sympathy or the slightest compassion. Mandelstam collects missteps.'

'Stalin, who never pardoned him for his poem, has been impervious to the ode he dedicated to him.'

'Might as well swallow his vomit.'

The poet who continues to die moves restlessly on his wooden bed.

His memory is playing tricks on him. Might as well grab a cloud.

Why did he agree to go to Samatikha?

The Writers' Residency was a trap. A prison.

The 'doctor' refused to let him go out at all.

To escape became an inner obsession that was never fulfilled from lack of means and energy.

He should have listened to Nadezhda and escaped when everyone was sleeping.

Unless he wanted to escape, Nadezhda convinced him not to.

Difficult in his condition to untangle the tangled knot of his memories.

Tossing on his board doesn't help the chronology of the facts.

His thoughts bring him back to Moscow each time he has trouble thinking. Moscow, which he couldn't do without.

Nadezhda and he escaped Voronezh as soon as they could, to breathe in the air of the city from which they were banished.

Back and forth during the day.

The last train took them to a deserted station. Ticket window closed and not a single traveller in sight.

The walk home. An hour's walk in the icy night.

The most difficult: walking on the bridge over the river, into a wind that barred their passage.

The same temptation for Mandelstam, suffocating, to throw himself into the icy water to be done with life.

Once home, their landlady, taking pity on them, gave them the remains of her meal.

Voronezh, a holiday destination compared to the hell of Samatikha.

That's what he's thinking now under his blanket which has become his shell.

It protects him from the guards who sort the deportees into two distinct categories: the dead, and the living.

The living-dead escape their classification.

A cadaver on the outside.

Only the arm that is raised during the distribution of bread is alive.

The cold, hunger, pain, no longer have a hold on him.

An emaciated body.

Hallucinations replace the absent flesh.

The end of the world is announced every morning by Fedor.

He escapes like the others. But he is the only one to use a bridge.

Arriving at the middle, he finds that it is cut off.

Impossible to go back, a barrier has just gone up behind him, he is now condemned to pass the rest of his existence with the sound of water.

An opaque, black water that rises, rises.

Finally drowning him.

Mandelstam regrets he never learnt how to swim.

The only student in the class not to join the others for that sort of activity.

The only one not to join with the others.

A rejection of their bourgeois milieu or the feeling of being different with his Jewish family?

The St Petersburg of his childhood. A world before the world, when he thinks about it now.

A silent childhood.

His father, a merchant, expressing himself only in numbers.

His mother silenced her sadness in the flat that smelt like dust and wilted roses.

His illiterate grandmother had shrunk her vocabulary to three words: 'Have you eaten?'

'Eat,' Nadezhda kept saying.

'Eat, you don't have any flesh on your bones.

'Chickpeas are rich in magnesium.

'Magnesium feeds the brain.

'Eat to be able to write.'

'Write for whom? I'm forbidden from publishing.'

'Write for yourself, for me, for our . . . why don't we have a child? A baby, a real one for both of us?'

'Yesterday you talked about a cow. Today a child. How would we feed it? Have you thought of that? Babies don't eat chickpeas. Babies don't have teeth.'

Unforgettable, Nadezhda's finger pointing to her wilting breast.

The living-dead man under his blanket laughs hysterically.

At night in their room in Voronezh.

The walls were closing in around Mandelstam as if to push him out. Difficult to go into the icy streets with the clothes given by the Writers' Union.

He paced around their fifteen square metres gesticulating.

Orating.

The overcoat inherited from a dead writer didn't protect him from the cold.

Death breathed its cold breath on his neck.

A shirt and not trousers, Gorky had decided.

With that, the great writer showed his contempt for avant-garde poetry.

Looking destitute.

The couple indifferent to their physical appearance.

Their minds preoccupied, above all, by food.

They were hungry. They were hungry all the time.

'Why don't we get a cow?'

Like the whistling of a train struggling up an incline, Nadezhda's leitmotif left Mandelstam without reaction.

'And what if we could find a less worn-out coat for you, a less moth-eaten blanket for the two of us, and something to eat other than chickpeas . . . '

Three fistfuls of chickpeas at every meal. The decision made by Nadezhda who held the strings of an empty purse.

Starving, badly dressed, they avoided mirrors so they wouldn't be ashamed of themselves.

There was no mirror in their room.

The only one they had ever had was lost during one of their five house moves. The murky shapes reflected by the glass of the store windows was theirs and yet not theirs.

The only recognizable elements, the boots made from Nadezhda's mother's old yellow leather trunk.

The former, always well-dressed student at the prestigious Tenischev School in St Petersburg thirty years earlier, now looks like a beggar.

His mother wanted her son to become a member of the elite.

He left school a revolutionary.

From his childhood in the cold city on the Volga, Mandelstam remembers the blocks of ice as tall as icebergs floating down the river as soon as the snow began to melt.

Remembers old Gorky holding onto the arm of his ageing wife.

He was in love with Lydia Zinovieva, the most beautiful girl in the city.

Her death left him devastated.

His encounter with Marina Tsvetaeva a year later, didn't heal the wound.

Marina's wild charm, her brutal words, her incandescent poems moved him and frightened him at the same time.

> *You throw back your head, because*
> *you are proud. And a braggart.*
> *This February has*
> *brought me a gay companion!*

—she wrote after they met.

The fantastic Tsvetaeva had been seduced by Mandelstam's long eyelashes touching his eyebrows but not by the rest of him.

Mandelstam introduced her to St Petersburg, she introduced him to Moscow through her body.

Tsvetaeva's voice, her gestures, her experience, obsessed him an entire summer.

He transported them to the cold city divided by the Volga the way his poems were divided between eroticism and Marxism.

Marxism: in 1917, he truly believed in it before changing his mind:

'The revolution declares the end of culture, the Party is the opposite of a church, the same authority and same subordination to a God. Man for them doesn't exist. He is only cement, bricks to construct from him, not for him.'

A declaration against the current of what adherents to Communism thought.

Overnight Mandelstam became a person of interest.

Marina Tsvetaeva became a person of interest, too, since her husband Sergei Efron had joined the Whites to fight against the Reds.

Also of interest, the great Akhmatova.

Her husband, the poet Gumilev, shot.

Her son Lev deported.

Akhmatova was one of the undesirables.

Stalin had decided to purge the country of all those who didn't adhere to his politics.

Villages in Siberia were emptied to be able to make way for the newly deported.

During a walk in the countryside not far from Saviolovo, Mandelstam and Nadezhda discovered an empty village.

All the inhabitants deported.

Only the cemetery was inhabited.

Entire families disappeared, the need to get rid of witnesses, the NKVD had decided.

Forty thousand dead windows
stare from all directions, there.

Two lines written in 1931 return to him while he is sleeping.

Mandelstam murmurs them in his sleep.

He is in a cemetery in the afternoon.

A man is following him. He feels his breath on his neck.

He knows it is Stalin but, unlike the time before, he isn't afraid.

'Do you hear your voice reciting your poem?'

'What's wrong with my voice?'

'It doesn't exist, I'm the only one who can hear it, given that you haven't stopped speaking to me for almost thirty years.'

All we hear is the Kremlin mountaineer
the murderer and peasant-slayer

'That's what you said before retracting it.

'Your ode to Stalin made me laugh.

'You write the way one lies.

'To be given a piece of pork and a bowl of soup.

'Shame on you, Mandelstam. You have debased yourself for nothing.

'Having become your obsession, I've fed your writing by not feeding you.

'Eternally starving, the Mandelstam couple. Two beggars.

'I will end up believing that you are hungry for me, that you would eat me, if necessary.

'The eater of men, eaten by a mosquito.

'Ha ha ha ha.'

Mandelstam is awakened by Stalin's tempestuous laughter.

Mandelstam's thoughts like the stopped hands of a watch.

They take him endlessly to his second arrest three years earlier.

Had he chosen Samatikha of his own volition, or had he been forced to go there?

Having returned from three years of exile in Voronezh, the couple remained undesirable in the capital.

Ordered to leave the city in twenty-four hours.

But Mandelstam always put off their departure until the next day.

The fear of being arrested during the night made him sleep at Shklovsky's place.

The sound of the lift stopping on every floor.

That of the cars in the street terrorizes him.

He goes home.

Throws himself into the mouth of the wolf.

Two knocks on the door.

An ordinary morning.

Nadezhda in her robe opens the door to the doctor and two men.

Used to arrests, she prepares a small bag with a change of underclothes.

'No need for a bag,' they reassure her.

'We'll bring him back shortly.

'Just the time it takes to ask a few questions.'

Not quite awake, Nadezhda realizes the horror of the situation once her husband is put in the van parked in front of their door.

When she visits him in prison, she learns that he has been sentenced to five years of forced labour for counter-revolutionary activity in a place of exile of his choice.

Outside a radius of at least 150 kilometres from Moscow.

All the potential cities are reviewed with their friends.

They don't know where to go.

What to choose between Kolomna, known for its raids.

Stavelovo, where they throw together criminals and common thieves.

Alexandrov, which smells like carrion, an open road to Siberia.

Mekles, where those who believe they have served their sentences arrive again, deported to another hell.

Was the choice of Samatikha due to its train station?

Two hours in the train to get to Moscow.

Moscow which continues to fascinate them despite the humiliations they had endured there.

Despite the defections of their former friends.

Only Shklovsky continued to open his door to them.

To give them shelter and food.

And to slip them a few roubles each time they stopped by.

Samatikha, suggested to Mandelstam as a Residency, proved to be the worst of all prisons.

The Writers' Residency is only an obligatory place of passage on the way to Siberia.

All requests to go out are refused.

Surrounded by snitches.

Watched day and night.

The couple is tempted to escape but has no means of transportation to leave the place.

Weakened by illness, Mandelstam is incapable of going twenty-five kilometres on foot.

No point in thinking about the train.

The trains that use the station are reserved for deportees piled up like cattle in windowless carriages.

'Stalin skimmed the country like the skin on milk,' wrote Nadezhda in her memoirs.

'Stalin doesn't need to cut off heads, they fall off themselves,' said Mandelstam.

'Systematic extermination of a certain category of individuals.'

Raids sometimes stopped.

People breathed, walked in the streets without sticking to the walls, due to overpopulated prisons.

Those shot giving up their places to new offenders.

Arrests started up again.

Mandelstam, in his rare moments of lucidity, when his heart stops tormenting him, thinks of the intellectuals and artists who disappeared overnight.

A good number of them were holding poems he had written himself.

Or had been transcribed by Nadezhda, who spent her time recopying and distributing.

Dissimulate, hide, make yourself invisible.

'Take off your hat. You'll be noticed,' she repeated to him each time they were in the street.

Every Soviet citizen was a suspect by definition.

Nadezhda speaks of a young violinist deported without reason but who never complained.

Denounced by his wife and children so they wouldn't meet the same fate, he went along the Volga.

Playing at weddings and celebrations to earn a living.

Cheerful, smiling, he endured the exile as long as he had his violin.

But committed suicide the day they confiscated it for making noise at night when he was playing at a village festival.

He was found hanging from a beam.

Nadezhda also mentions a singer who followed her husband from exile to exile.

He was in a forced-labour camp.

She earned a living through singing.

Separated for thirty years she waited for him to be freed.

Growing old didn't frighten her.

He would love her again when they were once again united under the same roof.

Freed, the man had just enough time to see his wife again through his tears.

Arrested again even when they had just informed him of the end of his exile.

Deported to another city.

Mandelstam under his blanket has trouble remembering the happy moments of his life.

His memory has erased the house of his childhood with its furniture, curtains, rugs, keeping only the tears of his mother playing the piano.

From Voronezh, he does not remember the goldfinch that enchanted him, but the cat that ate the bird before disappearing.

Attracted by misfortune, Mandelstam destroys, destroys himself.

'Man is made for happiness like a bird is made to fly,' Pasternak told him in a letter. But the two poets were not made from the same clay.

'Is he dead, is he alive?' his camp neighbours ask themselves every morning.

They talk of the same man, of the living cadaver whose bit of bread they all share.

Two black stones at the bottom of a well, Mandelstam's eyes when he manages to open them.

A dead branch, his emaciated arm raised by his neighbour to take his ration of bread.

Mandelstam didn't know that it took so much effort to open his eyes, didn't know he was incapable of raising his hand.

Dead on the outside while he continues to ask:

'Should I have granted importance to signs?

'Become superstitious to avoid catastrophe?'

How to explain their blanket found in tatters after their stay in Zadonsk?

The diluted ink of his poems hidden in the pillow?

Should he have taken Nadezhda's terror when she dreamt of icons seriously?

Destiny kept them on guard.

Preoccupied with daily life, they didn't listen to it.

Less tortured by hunger, cold, the fear of being arrested, they would have manoeuvred better, acted while considering the times instead of opposing the most powerful man in the country.

What could his pen do against the NKVD?

What could a single man do against the all-powerful dictator?

His well-aligned words didn't constitute an army.

His words were as poor, as powerless as he.

Incapable of protecting himself from Stalin who burst into all his nightmares.

He has returned to Moscow.

Empty streets.

No lights in the windows.

Doors bang in the wind.

The sound of boots strikes the night behind him, in front of him, around him.

A sound that reverberates on all the walls of the city.

On the high walls of the Kremlin before crumbling on Red Square.

Out of the darkness emerges a kepi, bushy eyebrows, a moustache.

'Where are the others?' Mandelstam asks the kepi, the eyebrows, the moustache.

'In Siberia, gone willingly. Left without you. They have abandoned you. Not one grocery store or restaurant left to feed you.

'You'll die of hunger.

'You'll endure the same fate, nothing for you to eat, either. Not a sheep or a chicken in sight, no fruit on trees, either.

'Anyway, there are no more trees, dead for lack of being cared for, watered, pruned.

'All the gardeners shot or deported to Siberia.

'Only the two of us left in the country. Condemned to devour each other.'

A grimace of disgust on Stalin.

'Unpalatable as you are, I won't attempt it.

'Hard flesh, tough skin, bloodless.

'You are dead, Mandelstam, but you don't know it. Raising a hand to take a piece of bread does not transform a dead man into a living one.

'And tell yourself that the one you called a man-eater doesn't eat cadavers.

'Consider yourself dead from this day forward.

'Stalin grants you permission to die.'

The same day, Nadezhda's package to Mandelstam is sent back with the note 'Return to sender. Recipient deceased.'

It was 27 December 1938.

Mandelstam thrown into a common grave.

Pushkin buried in great secret during a night filled with snow. Frost crunched under the steps of his pallbearers.

Not being able to bury her dead husband, Nadezhda went around to those who were keeping his poems to gather them.

For twenty years, she would travel the country looking for survivors of the transit camp of Vladivostok, those who might have witnessed the death of her husband.

How to determine the true from the false when the facts go back in time and the few witnesses' brains have been injured because no one gets out of the camp unscathed, wonders Nadezhda.

'Death was the only possible way out, given the inhumane conditions of detention,' says one survivor.

'Sent to Kolyma by sea when the bay was frozen the prisoners died during the crossing. Mandelstam was one of them,' another asserts.

Another speaks of barges filled to the brim with men, dynamited as soon as they were on the sea.

A survivor says he had known a mad, old man who recited his poems in a cave where the criminals and thieves gathered, the only ones who liked his poetry.

Only the account of a certain Kazarnovski who had served his sentence in Kolyma seemed believable to Nadezhda.

After escaping from the gulag, he wandered the country without a housing permit, without a bread card, hid to escape the militia, drowned his fear in alcohol. Walked day and night on bare feet.

Nadezhda gave him her mother's rubber boots.

'They were his size—his toes were frozen, he cut them off with an axe to avoid gangrene.'

Kazarnovski, who lived in the same barracks as Mandelstam, tells of a man who no longer had all his wits.

'He froze in his leather coat which by now was in tatters . . . he scarcely ate anything, and was afraid to . . . he never knew which was his own mess can . . . had been too badly beaten by the guards . . . was convinced that that his life would be made easier when Romain Rolland wrote to Stalin about him.'

Another detail: Mandelstam begged Kazarnovski, if ever he was freed, to find Nadezhda and to intervene with the Literary Foundation so it would help her.

'Attached to writers' organizations like a convict to his ball and chain, throughout his life Mandelstam couldn't obtain a piece of bread without their permission,' wrote Nadezhda bitterly.

Thirty years later, while she was fighting to get his name cleared, she discovered albums of Mandelstam's poems that had circulated from camp to camp and from cell to cell.

In one of those cells, the prisoners condemned to death had scratched two verses from her husband's poem on a wall:

Do I really exist
And will death come one day?

A Note on the Text

The two recurring lines that Vénus Khoury-Ghata cites as a leitmotif in this volume,

> All we hear is the Kremlin mountaineer,
> The murderer and peasant-slayer

are from the first version of the poem on Stalin. Nadezhda Mandelstam mentions this in her memoirs, *Hope against Hope*, translated by Max Hayward (New York: Modern Library, 1999).

The final version of the poem, written is November 1933, which led to his arrest in May 1934 is as follows:

> We live, not feeling the ground under our feet,
> no one hears us more than a dozen steps away,
>
> And when there's enough for half a small chat—
> ah, we remember the Kremlin mountaineer:
>
> Thick fingers, fat like worms, greasy,
> words solid as iron weights,

Huge cockroach-whiskers laughing,
boot-tops beaming.

And all around him a rabble of thin-necked
     captains:
he toys with the sweat of half-men.

Some whistle, some meow, some snivel,
he's the only one looking, jabbing.

He forges decrees like horseshoes—decrees and
     decrees:
This one gets it in the balls, that one in the
     forehead, him right between the eyes.

Whenever he's got a victim, he glows like a
     broad-chested
Georgian munching a raspberry

—Quoted from *Complete Poetry of Osip Emilevich Mandelstam* (Burton Raffel and Alla Burago trans) (Albany: State University of New York Press, 1973), p. 228.

Translator's Notes

The majority of Osip Mandelstam's poems that Khoury-Ghata cites in the original French text have been translated into English and can be found in this invaluable work: *Complete Poetry of Osip Emilevich Mandelstam*, translated by Burton Raffel and Alla Burago (Albany: State University of New York Press, 1973). For some of the other poems, I have quoted the English counterparts from published sources. In the rare instances where translations are not available, I have translated directly from the French versions.

PAGE 3 • 'All we hear is the Kremlin mountaineer . . . peasant-slayer'—Osip Mandelstam, *Complete Poetry of Osip Emilevich Mandelstam*, p. 228.

PAGE 5 • 'Cassandra, sweet-singing Cassandra . . . on every-one?'—Mandelstam, *Complete Poetry*, p. 110.

PAGE 6 • 'What had I wanted to say? I forgot . . . sing in unconsciousness'—Mandelstam, *Complete Poetry*, p. 188.

PAGE 16 • 'I've become afraid of living life . . . a nameless stone'—as quoted in Clare Cavanagh, *Osip Mandelstam and the Modernist Creation of Tradition* (Princeton University Press, 1994), p. 35.

PAGE 21 • 'All day long, damp autumn air . . . *my black purse!*'—Mandelstam, *Complete Poetry*, p. 50.

PAGE 23 • 'Huge cockroach-whiskers laughing . . . munching a raspberry'—Mandelstam, *Complete Poetry*, p. 228.

PAGES 24–5 • 'From his point of view . . . by higher authority' —Nadezhda Mandelstam, *Hope against Hope: A Memoir* (Max Hayward trans.) (New York: Modern Library, 1999), p. 235.

PAGE 31 • 'They led you away at dawn . . . children were crying'—Anna Akhmatova, *The Complete Poems of Anna Akhmatova* (Roberta Reeder trans.) (Brookline, MA: Zephyr Press, 2000), p. 386.

PAGE 32 • 'An idol is idle . . . tied in a knot'—Mandelstam, *Complete Poetry*, p. 254.

PAGE 34 • 'The silver coin melts . . . and what was his'— Paul Celan, *No One's Rose* (David Young trans.) (Grosse Pointe Farms, MI: Marick Press, 2014), p. 147.

PAGE 36 • 'I drank a toast in spirit . . . we can only steer clear'—Osip Mandelstam, *Journey to Armenia* (Sidney Monas trans.) (Devon: Notting Hill Editions, 2011), p. 57.

PAGE 40 • 'The usual reaction . . . jeers for the victim'— Nadezhda Mandelstam, *Hope against Hope*, p. 28.

PAGE 40 • 'this hard-living people . . . nailed to earth'— Mandelstam, *Complete Poetry*, pp. 184–5.

PAGE 44 • 'We have a spider-work . . . when I die'—Mandelstam, *Complete Poetry*, p. 211.

PAGE 45 • 'My eyelashes sting. . . A storm's coming'—Mandelstam, *Complete Poetry*, p. 192.

PAGE 52 • 'Distance: versts, miles . . . it unites us'—Marina Tsvetaeva, *Bride of Ice: New Selected Poems* (Elaine Feinstein trans.) (Manchester: Carcanet Press, 2009), p. 120.

PAGE 80 • 'A stone having rolled down . . . a sentient hand'—Quoted from Clarence Brown, *Mandelstam* (Cambridge: Cambridge University Press, 1978), p. 144.

PAGE 84 • 'I could not feel your image . . . an empty cage'—Mandelstam, *Complete Poetry*, p. 46.

PAGE 99 • 'You throw back your head . . . a braggart'—Tsvetaeva, *Bride of Ice*, p. 25.

PAGE 101 • 'Forty thousand dead windows . . . directions, there'—Mandelstam, *Complete Poetry*, p. 201.